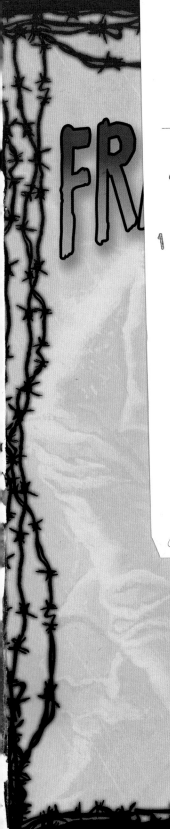

BASED UPON THE WORKS OF
MARY SHELLEY

FRANKENSTEIN

ABOUT THE AUTHOR

Mary Wollstonecraft Godwin was born in London, England, on 30 August, 1797. She was the only child of William Godwin and Mary Wollstonecraft. Both of her parents were writers. Her mother died soon after her birth. Mary's father remarried and she grew up with her sister and step-sister.

Mary and her sisters were educated at home by tutors. She read from her father's extensive library. She also wrote her own stories.

In 1812, Mary met the author Percy Bysshe Shelley and his wife Harriet. During the next couple of years, the three spent a lot of time together. Mary and Percy soon fell in love, and in 1814 they eloped to France. They were married two years later after Harriet died. Mary and Percy had a son, Percy Florence Shelley.

During their marriage, the Shelleys travelled and continued to write. Mary wrote her best-known work, *Frankenstein*, in 1818. In 1822, Percy Shelley died. Mary and her son returned to London, where Mary continued to write. On 1 February, 1851, Mary Shelley died in London.

"DEAR MARGARET..."

"OUR JOURNEY TO THE NORTH POLE HAS TAKEN A *STRANGE* AND RATHER *DRAMATIC* TURN."

"LAST MONDAY WE RAN INTO ICE WHICH QUICKLY SURROUNDED OUR SHIP ON ALL SIDES."

"THE ICE GOES ON FOR *MILES*. THE SIGHT WOULD BE A WONDER, DEAR SISTER, IF IT WERE NOT SUCH A TRIAL."

"BUT THERE WERE OTHER WONDERS."

CAPTAIN WALTON, *LOOK!*

BEFORE I BOARD, I MUST KNOW: *WHERE ARE YOU GOING?*

"OUT ON THE ICE WE FOUND A HALF-FROZEN MAN."

"GIVEN WHERE WE WERE, YOU CAN ONLY IMAGINE MY SURPRISE AT THIS QUESTION."

"I ANSWERED AND HE LET US BRING HIM ABOARD."

"HE COLLAPSED INTO BED. WE THOUGHT HE WOULD SURELY DIE."

"HE LIVED."

"AS SOON AS HE WOKE, HE INSISTED ON LEAVING HIS BED AND WENT UP TO THE SHIP'S DECK. HE PACED THERE FOR HOURS, LOOKING OUT TO SEA."

"HE CALLS HIMSELF VICTOR FRANKENSTEIN."

"WHEN ASKED WHY HE CAME TO THIS PLACE OF *COLD AND ICE*, HIS ANSWER SHOCKED US ALL."

"'TO FIND THE *DEMON* - AND *DESTROY HIM*,' HE SAID."

"FOR DAYS HE SPOKE OF NOTHING ELSE - AND WE FEARED HE HAD GONE MAD."

"BUT OBSESSION AND MADNESS ARE NOT ALWAYS THE SAME, MARGARET. I WAITED FOR HIM TO TELL HIS TALE."

I WAS BORN ABROAD, IN ITALY...

"THE FRANKENSTEIN FAMILY WAS AMONG THE MOST WELL KNOWN IN ALL GENEVA. OUR NAME GAVE US *PRIDE* AND EARNED US *RESPECT*."

"THOUGH MY PARENTS WORKED HARD, THEY TRAVELLED OFTEN."

"MY MOTHER CAME FROM A POOR FAMILY, AND UNDERSTOOD THE SUFFERING OF THE POOR. SHE OFTEN HELPED THEM, EVEN WHEN ABROAD."

"ONE SUCH FAMILY HAD FIVE CHILDREN TO FEED, INCLUDING A LITTLE GIRL."

"FOR MY MOTHER, IT WAS LOVE AT FIRST SIGHT. SHE LOVED ME WITH ALL HER HEART, BUT HAD ALWAYS WANTED A DAUGHTER, TOO."

"WHEN MY PARENTS SUGGESTED THEY ADOPT THE GIRL, BOTH THE COUPLE AND THE PARISH PRIEST AGREED."

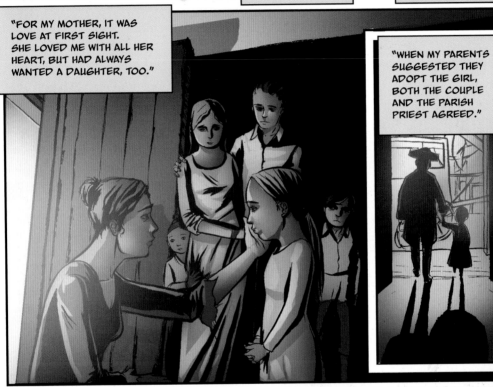

"HER NAME WAS ELIZABETH. MY PARENTS KNEW THAT WE WOULD BE CLOSE."

"INDEED, FROM THAT FIRST MOMENT I LOVED HER WITH ALL MY HEART. AND I VOWED TO *PROTECT* AND *CHERISH* HER ALWAYS."

"SOON AFTER, MY FAMILY RETURNED TO GENEVA, AND MY BROTHER WILLIAM WAS BORN."

"WHILE MY PARENTS LOOKED AFTER THE NEW BABY, I THREW MYSELF INTO MY STUDIES."

"INDEED, I HAD ONLY ONE REAL FRIEND. THOUGH MY SERIOUS NATURE HID IT WELL, I ADORED HENRY CLERVAL."

"HE WAS ALWAYS SO FULL OF LIFE. AS FOR ME, I LONGED TO FIND OUT LIFE'S *SECRETS*. I WANTED TO KNOW THE WORKINGS OF NATURE..."

"I HATED CROWDS AND I HAD FEW FRIENDS."

"...THE *SOUL OF MAN*, AND THE *SPIRIT OF LIFE ITSELF*."

"ONE EVENT STANDS OUT IN MY MEMORY..."

"DURING A STORM, I WATCHED AS AN OAK TREE DISAPPEARED IN A LIGHT FROM THE HEAVENS."

"WHEN I LEARNED WHAT A POWERFUL FORCE THE LIGHTNING WAS, I KNEW THAT SCIENCE WAS MY FUTURE. I HAD TO UNDERSTAND THE MYSTERIES OF LIFE..."

"IT WAS IN RIBBONS WHEN WE FOUND IT THE NEXT MORNING."

"...AND *DEATH*. OF *CREATION* AND *DESTRUCTION*."

"WHEN I WAS 17, ELIZABETH FELL ILL WITH SCARLET FEVER. HER YOUTH GAVE HER THE STRENGTH TO FIGHT AND SHE RECOVERED FULLY."

"MY MOTHER, WHO CARED FOR HER, DID NOT."

"IN HER FINAL MOMENTS, MOTHER GAVE US HER LAST WISHES."

YOUR UNION BEGAN LONG AGO, VICTOR AND ELIZABETH. MY CHILDREN, YOU MUST GET MARRIED.

"AND SO OUR *FATES* WERE INDEED SEALED. IT WAS OUR MOTHER'S LAST WISH."

"SHE GAVE US A GIFT BY SAYING WHAT WE HAD LEFT UNSPOKEN FOR YEARS."

"NOT LONG AFTER HER DEATH, I LEFT FOR UNIVERSITY AT INGOLSTADT."

"THERE, I MET TWO PROFESSORS WHO CHANGED THE COURSE OF MY STUDIES AND MY *DESTINY*..."

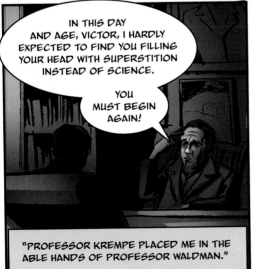

IN THIS DAY AND AGE, VICTOR, I HARDLY EXPECTED TO FIND YOU FILLING YOUR HEAD WITH SUPERSTITION INSTEAD OF SCIENCE.

YOU MUST BEGIN AGAIN!

"PROFESSOR KREMPE PLACED ME IN THE ABLE HANDS OF PROFESSOR WALDMAN."

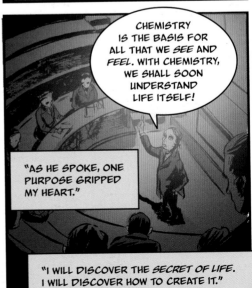

CHEMISTRY IS THE BASIS FOR ALL THAT WE *SEE* AND *FEEL*. WITH CHEMISTRY, WE SHALL SOON UNDERSTAND LIFE ITSELF!

"AS HE SPOKE, ONE PURPOSE GRIPPED MY HEART."

"I WILL DISCOVER THE *SECRET OF LIFE*. I WILL DISCOVER HOW TO CREATE IT."

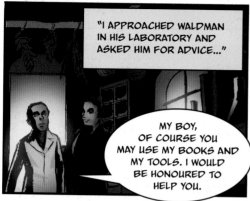

"I APPROACHED WALDMAN IN HIS LABORATORY AND ASKED HIM FOR ADVICE..."

MY BOY, OF COURSE YOU MAY USE MY BOOKS AND MY TOOLS. I WOULD BE HONOURED TO HELP YOU.

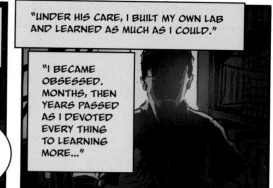

"UNDER HIS CARE, I BUILT MY OWN LAB AND LEARNED AS MUCH AS I COULD."

"I BECAME OBSESSED. MONTHS, THEN YEARS PASSED AS I DEVOTED EVERY THING TO LEARNING MORE..."

"BODY AFTER BODY I CUT OPEN TO FIND OUT HOW TO GIVE THE *SPARK OF LIFE* TO AN EMPTY SHELL..."

THE SECRET OF CREATION... THIS WOULD BE THE REWARD OF MY HARD WORK!"

"I DECIDED TO CREATE A MAN. I WOULD GIVE HIM LIFE, JUST LIKE A FATHER. AND LIKE A FATHER, I WOULD RECEIVE HIS LOVE COMPLETELY."

"I WORKED WITHOUT REST FOR MANY MONTHS."

"AND ON A DREARY NIGHT IN NOVEMBER, IT WAS TIME..."

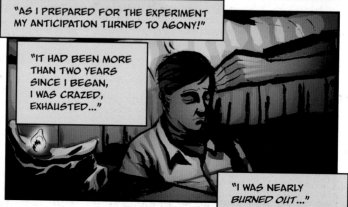

"AS I PREPARED FOR THE EXPERIMENT MY ANTICIPATION TURNED TO AGONY!"

"IT HAD BEEN MORE THAN TWO YEARS SINCE I BEGAN, I WAS CRAZED, EXHAUSTED..."

"I WAS NEARLY *BURNED OUT*..."

"BUT I WAS ALSO READY! READY TO INTRODUCE THE SPARK OF BEING - INTO THIS LIFELESS THING..."

ZZZZZT!!
ZZZZT!!

"BUT AFTER JUST ONE LOOK AT MY CREATION..."

"THE BEAUTY OF THE DREAM VANISHED. DISGUST AND HORROR FILLED MY HEART..."

"THE YELLOW SKIN... THE THING I HAD MADE WAS NOT HUMAN."

"UNABLE TO STAND THE SIGHT OF MY FAILURE, I RAN FROM THE LABORATORY."

"MORNING CAME AND I LOOKED FOR SAFETY ON THE STREETS OF INGOLSTADT."

"FEAR GRIPPED ME AS I WALKED. MAYBE THE HORRID THING HAD FOLLOWED ME..."

"IT HAD NOT. INSTEAD, A CHANCE MEETING WITH HENRY SAVED ME."

VICTOR! WHAT HAS HAPPENED, DEAR FRIEND?

DO NOT ASK, DO NOT SPEAK OF IT... OH I CANNOT BEAR IT.

"HENRY TOOK ME BACK TO HIS HOME."

VICTOR! WHAT IN GOD'S NAME IS THE MATTER?

DO NOT ASK ME. GOD CAN TELL. SAVE ME!

"I HAD THE BEGINNING OF A FEVER THAT WOULD LAST FOR MONTHS."

"HENRY ACCEPTED MY SILENCE, AND LOOKED AFTER ME LIKE I WAS HIS OWN SON."

"OH, I DID NOT DESERVE THIS."

"AS I GREW STRONGER, I PUT THE *MONSTER* OUT OF MY MIND."

"AND ALL THE WHILE, I SECRETLY PRAYED THAT THE *HORROR* WAS BEHIND ME."

"A LETTER FROM MY FATHER PROVED OTHERWISE."

"'HOW CAN I SPEAK OF SUCH HORRIBLE NEWS?' HE WROTE."

"'WILLIAM, YOUR SWEET BROTHER, IS DEAD. VICTOR, HE IS *MURDERED!*' HE WROTE."

"THE PRINT OF THE MURDERER'S FINGER WAS ON HIS NECK."

"THE WRETCH WAS THERE! THE FILTHY *DEMON* TO WHOM I HAD GIVEN LIFE! WHEN I SAW HIM, I KNEW THE *TRUTH.*"

"I RESOLVED TO VISIT THE VERY SPOT WHERE POOR WILLIAM HAD BEEN KILLED. I WENT TO GENEVA AT ONCE."

"THE CITY GATES WERE CLOSED BY THEN, LEAVING ME STRANDED IN THE MIDDLE OF A STORM."

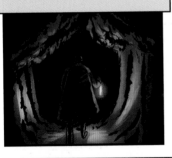

"HE WAS THE MURDERER! THERE WAS NO DOUBT."

"BUT A GOLD LOCKET OF WILLIAM'S WAS FOUND ON JUSTINE, A GIRL KEEPING ELIZABETH COMPANY WHILE I WAS AWAY."

"FLIMSY AS IT WAS, THE EVIDENCE WAS IMPOSSIBLE TO ARGUE. JUSTINE WAS *HUNG* FOR THE MURDER."

"AFTER THE EXECUTION, MY SADNESS ONLY GREW WORSE. FINALLY, MY FATHER SUGGESTED A TRIP TO THE FAMILY HOME."

"I TOOK TO THE MOUNTAINS, HOPING THE CLEAR AIR WOULD LIFT MY SPIRITS..."

"BUT I WAS TO FIND NO PEACE."

"HOW HAD HE FOLLOWED ME HERE? TRULY, I AM *CURSED!*"

DEVIL! HOW *DARE* YOU!

DO YOU NOT FEAR MY PUNISHMENT?

IF ONLY I COULD BRING YOUR VICTIMS BACK TO LIFE BY ENDING YOUR MISERABLE EXISTENCE!

HEAR ME OUT BEFORE YOU VENT YOUR HATRED. YOU *MADE ME!* I WILL BE GENTLE IF YOU TREAT ME SO.

NO! I WILL *NOT.* YOU ARE A VILLAIN.

LISTEN!

FRANKENSTEIN, I ASK YOU NOT TO *SPARE ME,* BUT ONLY TO LISTEN. ONLY THEN, IF YOU MUST, *DESTROY ME,* THE WORK OF YOUR OWN HANDS.

HEAR MY STORY AND DECIDE MY FATE.

"HE LED ME TO A CAVE OF ICE TO BEGIN HIS TALE."

"'MY EARLY DAYS ARE HARD TO REMEMBER,' SAID HE. 'COLD DARKNESS, THE WIND ON MY FACE, THE SOUNDS IN MY EARS... IT WAS A LONG TIME BEFORE I COULD TELL THEM APART.'"

"'BUT I REMEMBER THE DISCOVERY OF FIRE,' HE CONTINUED."

"I LOOKED FOR FOOD AND SHELTER, AND NOT KNOWING WHAT I DID, TOOK THESE AS I FOUND THEM."

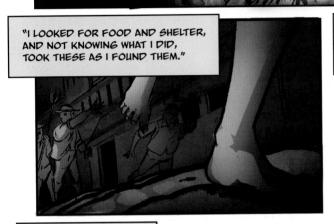

"SOON I LEARNED NOT TO STEAL. BUT EVERY PEASANT SCREAMED AT THE SIGHT OF ME."

"EVERYWHERE I WENT I FOUND ONLY HATRED."

"IT WAS CLEAR TO ME THAT I WOULD NEED TO HIDE TO SURVIVE. BUT I WAS SO *LONELY*."

"THOUGH I WAS HAPPY TO HAVE SHELTER FROM THE CRUELTY OF MEN, I STILL WANTED THEIR COMPANY..."

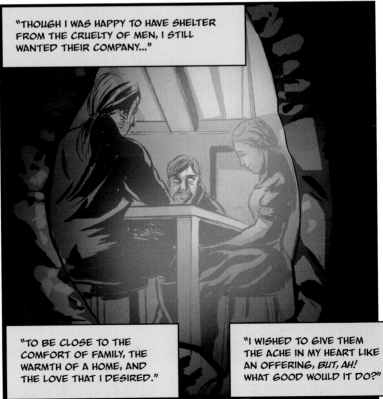

"TO BE CLOSE TO THE COMFORT OF FAMILY, THE WARMTH OF A HOME, AND THE LOVE THAT I DESIRED."

"I WISHED TO GIVE THEM THE ACHE IN MY HEART LIKE AN OFFERING, *BUT, AH!* WHAT GOOD WOULD IT DO?"

"I STARTED TO HELP A POOR FAMILY WHOSE FATHER WAS BLIND."

"THEN, ONE NIGHT I SAW MY REFLECTION IN A POOL OF WATER."

"AT FIRST, I COULD SCARCELY BELIEVE THAT I WAS THAT CREATURE. I HAD LONG ADMIRED THE PERFECT FORM OF THE POOR FAMILY."

"WHILE I COULD NOT SHED MY GHASTLY BODY, PERHAPS I COULD OVERCOME IT WITH ACTS OF KINDNESS, AND PERHAPS THESE ACTS SHOULD TOUCH OTHERS."

"BUT THERE IS NO HIDING FROM THE MONSTER THAT I AM."

FELIX, LOOK! COME QUICKLY!

"THIS WAS HIS ONLY SATISFACTION. HIS ONLY REWARD."

IT IS ENOUGH WOOD TO LAST US FOR SEVERAL DAYS! WHERE DID IT COME FROM?

I-IT... IT IS... EENUF...

"IT WAS DIFFICULT AT FIRST. BUT THEN I FOUND A BAG OF BOOKS. I LEARNED STEADILY."

"I WAS DETERMINED TO REACH THEM. AND FOR THAT, I NEEDED THEIR LANGUAGE."

"SOON IT WAS TIME TO COME OUT OF HIDING."

"MY MONSTER CONTINUED HIS STORY. 'THE BLIND MAN AND I CONNECTED IMMEDIATELY. HIS FONDNESS FOR ME GREW AS WE WAITED THE ARRIVAL OF HIS TWO CHILDREN.'"

"BUT THEY WERE MORE BLIND THAN HE."

MISERABLE WRETCH! GET OUT! **GET OUT!**

"SURELY HE WOULD HELP THEM TO UNDERSTAND ME. HELP THEM TO SEE."

"YOU CALL ME A *MURDERER*, BUT, YOU MUST KNOW THE TRUTH."

"I TRIED SO HARD TO HELP HUMANS."

"NOTHING COULD SOFTEN THEIR HARD, HARD HEARTS."

"A HEART OF STONE CLAMOURS FOR ONE THING: *REVENGE*."

"SOON MY OWN HEART BEGAN TO TURN...TO HARDEN..."

"YOUR BROTHER'S PREJUDICE SEALED HIS FATE, AND MINE."

CALM YOURSELF, CHILD. I SHALL NOT HURT YOU.

LET ME GO! MY FATHER IS VICTOR FRANKENSTEIN - LET ME GO OR HE WILL *PUNISH* YOU!

"HE LEFT ME NO CHOICE."

"AFTER IT WAS DONE, I FOUND A LOCKET ON YOUR BROTHER'S CHEST. THE WOMAN IN IT WAS THE MOST BEAUTIFUL CREATURE I HAD EVER SEEN."

"IN A NEARBY BARN, I SAW A WOMAN EVEN MORE BEAUTIFUL. I IMAGINED HER SMILE, WHAT JOY IT MUST BRING..."

"BUT NOT FOR ME. NEVER FOR ME! IF SHE WERE TO SEE ME, SURELY SHE WOULD CURSE ME. CALL ME A *MURDERER*..."

"A CREATURE I COULD NEVER HAVE."

"IT IS AS IT HAS ALWAYS BEEN."

"AFTER HE FINISHED TELLING HIS TALE, HE TURNED TO ME."

FOR SOME DAYS, I HAVE HAUNTED THIS SPOT. I HAVE BEEN CONSUMED WITH *RAGE* AND *PASSION* THAT ONLY YOU CAN SATISFY. YOU SHALL *DIE* HERE NOW UNLESS YOU MAKE ME A PROMISE.

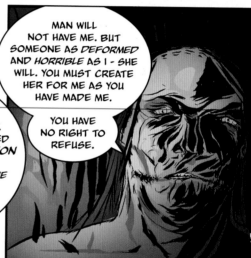

MAN WILL NOT HAVE ME. BUT SOMEONE AS *DEFORMED* AND *HORRIBLE* AS I - SHE WILL. YOU MUST CREATE HER FOR ME AS YOU HAVE MADE ME.

YOU HAVE NO RIGHT TO REFUSE.

"*HORRID!* YET, I KNEW HE WAS RIGHT. I COULD NOT REFUSE."

IF I DO THIS, YOU MUST SWEAR TOO. *SWEAR* THAT IT ENDS THEN.

I SWEAR BY THE SUN AND HEAVEN, AND BY THE FIRE THAT STILL *BURNS* IN MY HEART. IF YOU MAKE ME A MATE, NO MAN WILL *EVER* SEE ME AGAIN.

"IT WAS DONE."

"AND SO IT BEGAN. MY FATHER WISHED FOR ME TO MARRY SWEET ELIZABETH, BUT I WAS DETERMINED TO PUT AN END TO MY SLAVERY. ONCE AGAIN, I SHUT MYSELF AWAY."

"THREE YEARS AGO, I HAD CREATED THIS FIEND. HE HAS BROUGHT NOTHING BUT DEATH, SUFFERING AND MADNESS INTO THE WORLD."

"AS I WORKED, I COULDN'T HELP BUT REFLECT..."

"I NOW MAKE ANOTHER, NOT KNOWING HOW SHE WOULD BEHAVE."

"HE SAID HIS ACTS WERE REVENGE, BUT WHAT IF SHE MURDERED FOR ITS OWN SAKE?"

"WHAT IF THEY HAVE *CHILDREN*?"

"HE HAD SWORN TO HIDE, BUT SHE HAD NOT..."

"WHAT IF THEY HATE EACH OTHER?"

"*THIS IS MADNESS.*"

GRRAAHHH!!!

SLAVE! YOU THINK YOU ARE *MISERABLE*? I CAN MAKE YOU HATE THE VERY LIGHT OF DAY!

UNDERSTAND THAT YOU ARE MY CREATOR, BUT I AM NOW YOUR MASTER.

SHALL EACH BEAST HAVE HIS MATE AND I BE *ALONE*? ARE YOU TO BE HAPPY WHILE I SUFFER?

REMEMBER MY *STONE HEART* REMAINS, BEWARE, FOR I AM FEARLESS -

AND I SHALL BE WITH YOU ON YOUR WEDDING NIGHT.

"HIS WORDS RANG IN MY EARS LONG AFTER ALL WAS SILENT..."

"IMAGES OF MY OLD LIFE - MY FATHER, HENRY, MY BRIDE-TO-BE - SWIRLED IN THE DARKNESS. I RESOLVED TO FINISH THIS HORRID BUSINESS FOR GOOD."

"BUT THERE WAS ONE MORE TASK TO PERFORM."

"I WISH I COULD SAY THAT IT LIFTED MY BURDENS, BUT..."

"...FAR GREATER HORRORS AWAITED ME ONSHORE."

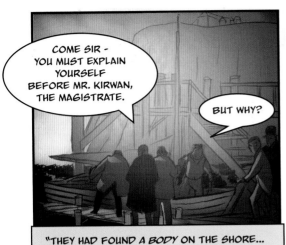

COME SIR - YOU MUST EXPLAIN YOURSELF BEFORE MR. KIRWAN, THE MAGISTRATE.

BUT WHY?

"THEY HAD FOUND A *BODY* ON THE SHORE... AND I HAD BEEN THE ONLY MAN IN SIGHT."

"A WOMAN WAITING FOR THE FISHERMEN TO RETURN SAID SHE SAW MY BOAT PUSH OFF SHORTLY BEFORE THE BODY WAS FOUND."

"THE BODY WAS NOT YET COLD WHEN THEY BROUGHT IT IN."

"THERE WAS NO SIGN OF VIOLENCE, SAVE FOR THE BLACK FINGER MARKS AT THE NECK."

"WHY DID I NOT *DIE?*"

"WAS I NOT A MURDERER MYSELF?"

"THE MOMENT THAT THEY PULLED BACK THE SHEET IS A NIGHTMARE FROM WHICH I *SWEAR* I SHALL NEVER WAKE. MY DEAR FRIEND HENRY WAS UNDERNEATH."

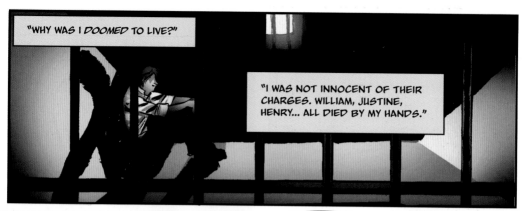

"WHY WAS I *DOOMED* TO LIVE?"

"I WAS NOT INNOCENT OF THEIR CHARGES. WILLIAM, JUSTINE, HENRY... ALL DIED BY MY HANDS."

"A JAIL CELL WAS BUT A SLIGHT PUNISHMENT FOR MY CRIMES."

WHOSE MURDER AM I RESPONSIBLE FOR THIS TIME?

FEAR NOT, SIR. YOUR FAMILY IS PERFECTLY WELL.

AND A FRIEND HAS COME TO VISIT YOU.

FATHER!!

I'VE COME TO TAKE YOU HOME, SON.

THEY HAVE NO EVIDENCE - THEY CANNOT HOLD YOU.

"WE SET SAIL FOR GENEVA SOON AFTER. BUT I KNEW THERE WOULD BE NO PEACE. AND I HAD BUT ONE JOB TO DO."

"TO WATCH OVER MY LOVED ONES, LAY IN WAIT FOR THE MURDERER AND PUT AN END TO HIM."

"I WOULD NOT *SLEEP*. I WOULD NOT *REST*."

GENEVA, MONTHS LATER.

"MY WEDDING TO ELIZABETH SHOULD HAVE BEEN A HAPPY TIME BUT IT WAS FILLED WITH *DREAD* FOR WHAT WAS TO COME."

"THE MONSTER HAD MADE A PROMISE. HE WOULD KEEP IT."

"I WAS VERY CAREFUL. I SENT MEN TO SURROUND THE FAMILY HOME, KEPT WEAPONS IN THE BRIDAL SUITE... AND DIDN'T TELL ELIZABETH A THING."

"AND WHEN THE CEREMONY WAS DONE ALL THAT WAS LEFT TO DO WAS WAIT."

VICTOR, WHAT'S WRONG? THERE IS NO SENSE IN HIDING YOUR DISTRESS. I SEE IT PLAINLY.

DO NOT ASK ME THESE THINGS, ELIZABETH.

IT'S TIME FOR BED NOW.

BUT VICTOR -

YES. GO TO OUR ROOM AND LOCK THE DOOR.

DO NOT OPEN IT FOR ANYONE. NO MATTER WHAT.

"I HATED TO LEAVE HER ALONE ON OUR WEDDING NIGHT."

AIEEEEE!

COME AND GET ME MONSTER. IT IS TIME TO KEEP YOUR WORD. AND IN TURN, I SHALL MAKE GOOD ON MINE.

IT ENDS HERE.

"BUT SHE MUST NOT SEE WHAT IS COMING."

"INDEED IT DID."

21

"AND THAT IS WHEN I FINALLY *UNDERSTOOD* THE DEPTHS OF MY SELF-DECEPTION..."

"THE MONSTER'S WEDDING NIGHT VISIT WAS NEVER MEANT FOR *ME*."

"HE MOUTHED WORDS THROUGH THE WINDOW. 'AND NOW WE ARE EVEN.'"

"A *STONE HEART* FOR A *STONE HEART*."

"AH, BUT HE UNDERESTIMATED ME."

BANG!!!

"I WOULD *MATCH* HIS RAGE. HIS THIRST FOR REVENGE."

"AT THAT MOMENT, WE WERE EVEN."

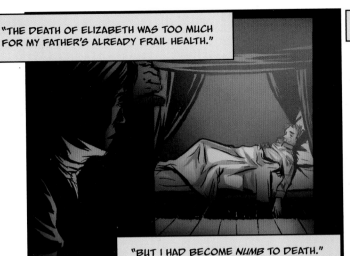

"THE DEATH OF ELIZABETH WAS TOO MUCH FOR MY FATHER'S ALREADY FRAIL HEALTH."

"BUT I HAD BECOME *NUMB* TO DEATH."

"A HEART OF STONE DOES NOT FEEL."

"I WOULD BEGIN A JOURNEY..."

BY THIS SACRED EARTH ON WHICH I DO KNEEL, HERE I DO *SWEAR*...

"...AND I WOULD NEED THE HELP OF MY VICTIMS. I VISITED THEM ONE LAST TIME."

TO *PURSUE* YOUR MURDERER TO THE ENDS OF THE EARTH, UNTIL HE IS DESTROYED.

HA HA HA

AND I CALL ON YOU, *SPIRITS OF THE DEAD*, TO AID ME IN THIS WORK.

A NOBLE AIM, CREATOR. ALAS, YOU SEEM DETERMINED TO LIVE...

FOR AS LONG AS YOU DO, THEY SHALL REMAIN UN-AVENGED.

NO!!

"I VOWED NOT TO REST UNTIL IT IS DONE. I SHALL FOLLOW HIM TO THE ENDS OF THE EARTH."

"THE *PURSUED* SHALL BECOME THE *PURSUER*."

"LET HIM THINK THAT HE IS BETTER THAN ME – HIS MAKER. LET HIM THINK HE CAN HIDE FROM ME."

"FOR I KNOW BETTER..."

"AND HE SHALL KNOW NO PEACE."

"THE BOAT HEADED NORTH, INTO THE ICE. A PLACE NOT FIT FOR MEN ON THIS EARTH. IT SEEMED FITTING THAT IT SHOULD END THERE."

"I MADE THE PREPARATIONS."

"HE LEFT HORROR WHEREVER HE WENT. LITTLE DID HE KNOW HOW EASY HE WAS TO FOLLOW."

"EACH TRACE OF HIM SPURRED ME ON TO THE NEXT..."

"IT WAS ONLY A MATTER OF *TIME*."

"AT THE END OF HIS STORY, DEAR MARGARET, THE MAN WAS WEAKER THAN EVER."

SWEAR THAT YOU WILL KEEP GOING. YOU MUST. IT IS IN YOUR HANDS NOW...

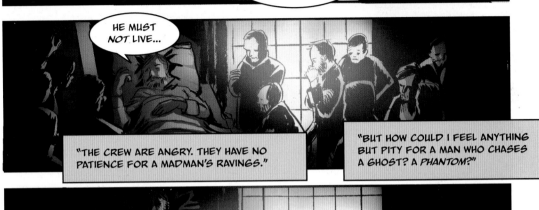

HE MUST NOT LIVE...

"THE CREW ARE ANGRY. THEY HAVE NO PATIENCE FOR A MADMAN'S RAVINGS."

"BUT HOW COULD I FEEL ANYTHING BUT PITY FOR A MAN WHO CHASES A GHOST? A *PHANTOM?*"

"IT MATTERED NOT, MARGARET. HIS CHASE HAS COME TO AN END WITH HIS LAST BREATH."

"THE ICE MELTS NOW, AND THE FOG HAS LIFTED."

"WE SHALL RETURN TO ENGLAND AT ONCE."

CRASH...

BOOOM

WHAT? WHO IS THERE?

AH, CREATOR. AH, FATHER!

SO LONG I HAVE DWELLED IN *DARKNESS*. ONLY NOW DO I SEE THE LIGHT OF DAY.

ONLY NOW... WHEN YOUR HEART BEATS NO MORE.

WHAT IS THIS *MADNESS*?

WHAT HAVE I *DONE*?

This edition first published in 2010 by
Franklin Watts
338 Euston Road
London NW1 3BH

Franklin Watts Australia
Level 17/207 Kent Street
Sydney NSW 2000

First published in the USA by Magic Wagon, a division of the ABDO Group

1 3 5 7 9 10 8 6 4 2

Original novel by Mary Shelley
Written by Elizabeth Genco
Illustrated by Jason Ho
Coloured and lettered by Jay Fotos
Edited and directed by Chazz DeMoss
Original cover design by Neil Klinepier
UK cover design by Peter Scoulding

A CIP catalogue record for this book is available from the British Library.

Dewey number: 741.5

ISBN: 978 0 7496 9683 2

Printed in China

Franklin Watts is a division of Hachette Children's Books,
an Hachette UK company.
www.hachette.co.uk

READ THE REST OF THIS STORY IN: PHANTOM OF THE OPERA